he Perfect Place for an Elf Owl

By the First and Second Grade Multiage Class

at Anthony T. Lane Elementary School

Scholastic Inc.
New York Toronto London Auckland Sydney Mexico City New Delhi Hong Kong Buenos Aires

One windy night in the desert, mama elf owl went out in search of dinner for her babies.

The youngest elf owl missed his mama and left his nest to find her.

A gust of wind blew him away.
He tumbled into the tundra.

4

The youngest elf owl missed his mama and left his nest to find her.

3

A gust of wind blew him away.
He tumbled into the tundra.

5

The owlet asked
a snowy owl,
"Is this my home?"

The snowy owl turned
its head and said,
"The tundra is no place
for an elf owl."
Just then, the wind
blew again.

Tundra Fact Box

The tundra is a perfect place for snowy owls.
The snowy owls' white feathers camouflage
them from prey. The feathers keep them warm
in the cold temperatures. There are not many
trees in the tundra, so snowy owls build their
nests on the ground. Snowy owls are diurnal.

The owlet fell into the forest.
He asked a spotted owl,
"Is this my home?"

8

Forest Fact Box

The forest is a perfect place for spotted owls. There are lots of trees so spotted owls can build their nests. They make their nests out of sticks which are all over the forest. Flying squirrels, mice and little birds live in the forest, too, and are good food for spotted owls.

The spotted owl blinked his eyes and said, "The forest is no place for an elf owl."

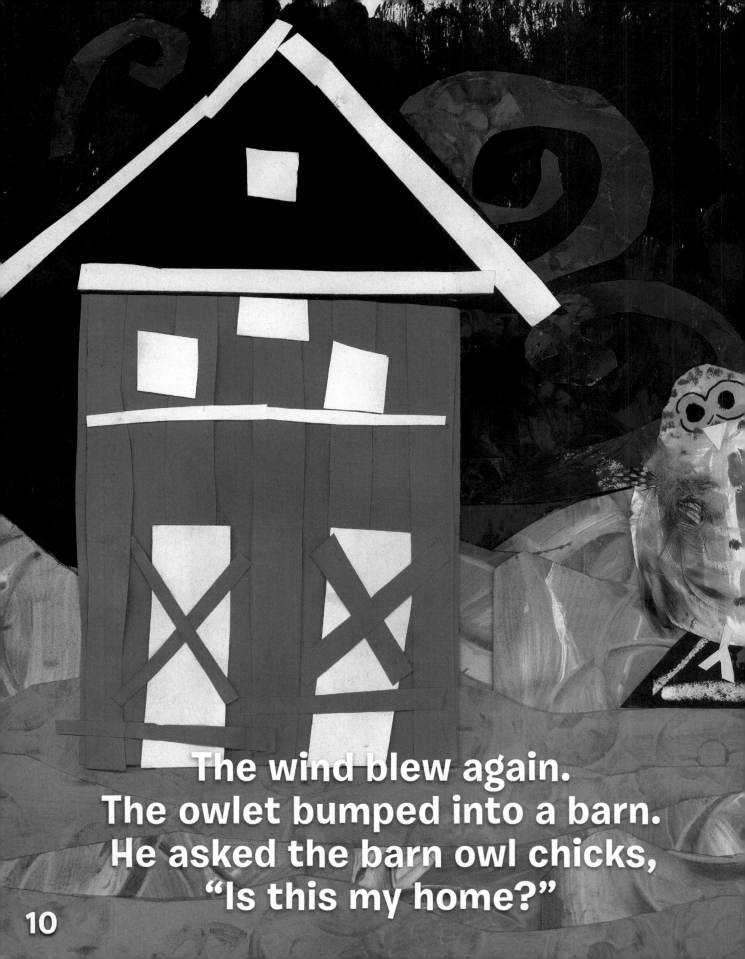

The wind blew again.
The owlet bumped into a barn.
He asked the barn owl chicks,
"Is this my home?"

Barn Fact Box

The barn is a perfect place for barn owls and their chicks. A barn has lots of mice that hide in the hay. Barn owls love to eat mice. A barn gives shelter to the barn owls. They build their nests in the rafters, which are high above any danger.

The barn owl chicks screeched, "A barn is no place for an elf owl."

A strong breeze blew.

The owlet bounced into a boreal forest.

Boreal Forest Fact Box

The boreal forest is a perfect place for boreal owls because the forest has prey like chipmunks and ground voles that are yummy to eat. Boreal owls can hide in the branches of a spruce tree.

He asked the
boreal owl,
"Is this my home?"
The boreal owl
said, "A boreal
forest is no place
for an elf owl."

The wind puffed.
The owlet ended up underground.

Underground Fact Box

The underground is a good place for burrowing owls because their predators cannot find them there. They come out during the day to hunt. Burrowing owls are diurnal.

16

He asked a burrowing owl,
"Is this my home?"
The burrowing looked
through the darkness and said,
"A burrow is no place for an
elf owl."

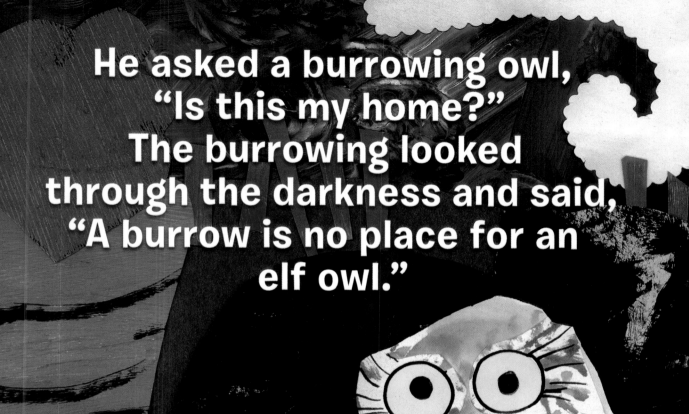

The wind blasted.

The owlet slipped into a swamp.

Swamp Fact Box

The swamp is a perfect place for barred owls. The swamp is squishy. Frogs and salamanders like wet places and they are the perfect prey for barred owls.

He asked a barred owl,
"Is this my home?"
The barred owl hooted, "The
swamp is no place for an elf owl."

21

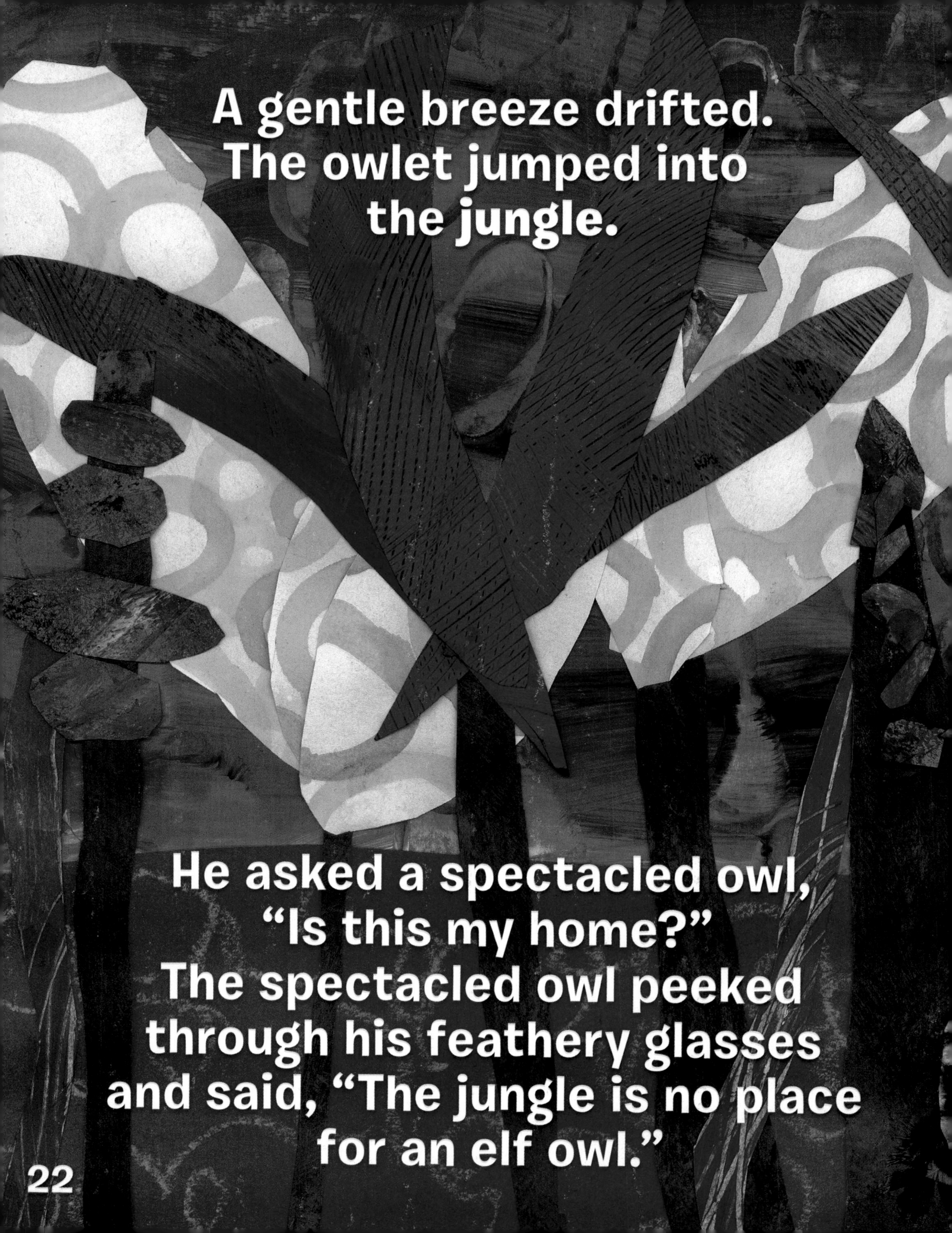

A gentle breeze drifted.
The owlet jumped into
the jungle.

He asked a spectacled owl,
"Is this my home?"
The spectacled owl peeked
through his feathery glasses
and said, "The jungle is no place
for an elf owl."

Jungle Fact Box

The jungle or rainforest is a perfect place for spectacled owls because there are small creatures like mice and lizards for them to eat. The jungle has tall trees that make good nesting places for spectacled owls.

The air burst into wind.
The wind dropped the owlet
into the **desert**.

Desert Fact Box

The desert is the perfect place for elf owls. When a gila woodpecker moves out of a saguaro cactus nest, an elf owl has a home in which to stay. The nest is comfortable because the water inside the cactus cools the nest like an air conditioner. There are a lot of desert mice, moths, centipedes, and scorpions around the saguaro cactus for elf owls to munch.

He asked the mama elf owl,
"Is this my home."
"Yes," said the mama owl,
"and you're late for dinner."
The owlet snuggled up
into the saguaro cactus.
He was home and he was happy.

The Perfect Way to make an Elf Owl Book

Kids Are Authors®
Books written by children for children

The Kids Are Authors® Competition was established in 1986 to encourage
children to read and to become involved in the creative process of writing.
Since then, thousands of children have written and illustrated books as participants
in the Kids Are Authors® Competition.

The winning books in the annual competition are published by Scholastic Inc.
and are distributed by Scholastic Book Fairs throughout the United States.

For more information:
Kids Are Authors® 1080 Greenwood Blvd., Lake Mary, FL 32746
Or visit our web site at: www.scholastic.com/kidsareauthors

ISBN-978-0-545-40292-7
12 11 10 9 8 7 6 5 4 3 2 1

Cover design by Bill Henderson
Printed and bound in the U.S.A.
First Printing, July 2011